# We're Going on a Treasure Hunt

Concept and pictures by **Tom Arma**

Written by Lenny Hort

**Harry N. Abrams, Inc., Publishers**

Designer: Allison Henry

The illustrations for this book were created using a blend of photography and other techniques.

No babies (or animals) were harmed in the making of We're Going on a Treasure Hunt.

Library of Congress Cataloging-in-Publication Data

Hort, Lenny.
  We're going on a treasure hunt / concept and pictures by Tom Arma ;
written by Lenny Hort.
      p. cm.
Summary: Babies in animal costumes visit a variety of undersea animals,
from starfish to crabs, in search of a treasure chest.
  ISBN 0-8109-4654-8
 (1. Babies—Fiction. 2. Marine animals—Fiction. 3. Treasure
hunts—Fiction.) I. Arma, Tom, ill. II. Title.

PZ7.H.7918Wg 2003
 (B)—dc21
                              200300733

Printed and bound in China
10 9 8 7 6 5 4 3 2 1

Visit Tom's Web site at www.tomarma.com

Abrams is a subsidiary of
LA MARTINIÈRE
G R O U P E

Harry N. Abrams, Inc.
100 Fifth Avenue
New York, N.Y. 10011
www.abramsbooks.com

For Julie Ann and Violet Rose
—T.A.

We're going on a treasure hunt.
We're going to the ocean.
We're going to look for treasure at the sandy beach.

Let's ask a **starfish**,
"Have you seen the treasure?"
"Have I seen the treasure?
No, not me!
Go and ask some **shellfish**
with **pinchy** little red **claws**
if you want to find the treasure in the sea."

Let's ask some stone crabs,

"Have you seen the treasure?"

"Have we seen the treasure?

No, not we!

Go and ask a creature

with a pearl in its shell

if you want to find the treasure in the sea."

Let's ask an oyster,
"Have you seen the treasure?"
"Have I seen the treasure?
No, not me!
Go and ask a giant
that leaps out of the water
if you want to find the treasure in the sea."

Let's ask a **whale**,

"Have you seen the treasure?"

"Have I seen the treasure?

No, not me!

Go and ask a **shellfish**

with **nutcracker claws**

if you want to find the treasure in the sea."

We're going on a treasure hunt.
We're going to the ocean.
We're going to look for treasure in the rippling waves.

Let's ask a lobster,
"Have you seen the treasure?"
"Have I seen the treasure?
No, not me!
Go and ask a mammal
that skips over the water
if you want to find the treasure in the sea."

Let's ask a dolphin,
"Have you seen the treasure?"
"Have I seen the treasure?
No, not me!
Go and ask a fish
that seems all set for riding
if you want to find the treasure in the sea."

Let's ask a seahorse,
"Have you seen the treasure?"
"Have I seen the treasure?
No, not me!
Go and ask a fish
that's the color of bananas
if you want to find the treasure in the sea."

Let's ask an angelfish,
"Have you seen the treasure?"
"Have I seen the treasure?
No, not me!
Go and ask a creature
with eight waving arms
if you want to find the treasure in the sea."

Let's ask an OCTOPUS,
"Have you seen the treasure?"
"Have I seen the treasure?
No, not me!
Go and ask a fish
that's the color of the sky
if you want to find the treasure in the sea."

Let's ask a blue fish,
"Have you seen the treasure?"
"Have I seen the treasure?
No, not me!
Go and ask a girl
with a fishy, swishy tail
if you want to find the treasure in the sea."

Let's ask a mermaid,
"Have you seen the treasure?"
"Have I seen the treasure?
No, not me!
Go and ask a creature
with a shell that curls around it
if you want to find the treasure in the sea."

We're going on a treasure hunt.
We're going to the ocean.
We're going to look for treasure by a sunken ship.

Let's ask a **sea snail**,

"Have you seen the treasure?"

"Have I seen the treasure?

No, not me!

Go and ask a **reptile** with a **shell** on its backside

if you want to find the treasure in the sea."

Let's ask a **turtle**,
"Have you seen the treasure?"
"Have I seen the treasure?
Look and see!"

We found it!

We all went on a
treasure hunt.
We all explored the ocean.
We all can share the treasure
from the deep blue sea.

# ARTIST'S NOTE

One of my favorite stories as a child was Jules Verne's *20,000 Leagues Under the Sea*. Later in life, and by then a big fan of Jacques Cousteau and his voyages on the *Calypso*, I began to research Verne and discovered that he had never actually ventured under the sea. In fact, in 1870, the year his nautical classic was published, deep-sea diving was pure fantasy.

Being a dedicated armchair traveler with an interest in sea life who also happens to be a baby photographer might not qualify me for a berth on the *Calypso*, but it certainly gave me the idea for *We're Going on a Treasure Hunt*, an underwater fantasy for the youngest adventurers.

With my last book, *We're Going on Safari*, I took the giant step from taking pictures to "making" pictures, using computer technology to go places I've only dreamed of, and taking "my" babies with me.

It all begins with the costume creation, followed by extensive casting where I might see five hundred babies for a single character. When I find the perfect baby, the fun begins. The baby comes to my studio with Mom, Dad, or grandparents, and I photograph him or her in costume. The whole shoot lasts perhaps five minutes.

To create most of the underwater worlds in *Treasure Hunt*, I had to build suitable environments for the babies. Some of these, like the treasure chest scene, were built from over a hundred different digital images. I use a small graphics tablet and two large monitors to assemble, paint, and blend the images, finishing the pictures with a special technique I have developed to give them the hyperreal look you see on these pages. Each picture can take weeks of experimentation to get it just the way I want it. It is all in the details—the ones you *don't* see.

Deep-sea exploration and searching for sunken treasure were certainly things of my childhood dreams. These—coupled with my love of creatures both above and below the waterline—made *Treasure Hunt* a real joy to create.

—Tom Arma